Simon and Schuster
First published in Great Britain in 2013 by Simon & Schuster UK Ltd
1st Floor, 222 Gray's Inn Road, London WC1X 8HB
A CBS Company

A CIP catalogue record for this book is available from the British Library
ISBN   978-1-47111-909-5
Printed and bound in Slovakia, TBB, a.s.
10 9 8 7 6 5 4 3 2 1

www.despicable.me
www.simonandschuster.co.uk

The Junior Novel

Adapted by Annie Auerbach
With Contributions by Brett Hoffman
Based on the Motion Picture Screenplay
Written by Cinco Paul & Ken Daurio

SIMON AND SCHUSTER

Prologue

I n the Arctic Circle, there is snow and ice as far as the eye can see. And, man, is it cold! There's not a lot to do; even if you're a Russian guard at a top secret research laboratory, time still passes slowly. Unless...you have a deck of cards!

Using an overturned barrel as a table, the guards engage in a serious card game. When one of them wins the game, he happily pulls the coins toward himself and does a celebratory dance, spinning around. When he finally stops dancing, however, he notices that his coins are gone!

He immediately accuses the other guard of

stealing them, but his opponent insists he didn't. All of a sudden, the metal barrel flies into the air!

The guards look up to see a gigantic magnetic ship hovering above the laboratory.

Suddenly, a lab door opens and a bunch of fellow guards rush out, pointing their guns at the magnetic ship.

WHOOSH! All of their guns are pulled up toward the ship, along with the guards themselves, who are strapped to the weapons!

Next, the entire lab begins to move off the ground. Terrified guards and scientists leap out into the snow below. With a final *clank*, the lab makes contact with the mysterious ship. As it flies away, the remaining guards and scientists watch with open mouths.

Three weeks later, top secret government agents view the security footage of the research station being magnetically stolen.

"We're still no closer to cracking this?" a portly man asks in an uptight British accent.

When there is no response, he gives an order: "Bring him in."

Chapter One

Gru surveys the scene in front of him. Yep, it's time. He grabs a menacing-looking weapon, pulls the trigger and...out comes a unicorn balloon! He puts it next to the other ones lining the windowsill and smiles, knowing they look just perfect for Agnes's sixth birthday party.

Not long after, the party is in full swing. The yard is decorated with balloons and streamers, along with a big bouncy house shaped like a castle. But this is no regular party with boring party games. This is a party thrown by Gru!

In one corner, two little girls fish in a small

kiddie pool. One of the girls gets a bite and happily pulls up a toy fish... until a real-life piranha jumps out and eats the toy fish! In another part of the yard, a boy and a girl sword fight. The boy does a bunch of fancy moves, but the girl is *not* impressed.

Agnes goes down a slide, a giant grin on her face. "This is the best party EVER!" she declares. Her friends are dressed as duchesses and countesses, while Agnes is dressed as a princess riding a unicorn, which is her favourite animal in the whole entire world!

Meanwhile, Edith is dressed as a ninja. She climbs across the monkey bars, just as a bunch of boxing gloves and spikes pop up from below. She avoids them with skill and ease. She then jumps to the ground, narrowly avoiding a bear trap.

"Ha-ha! Yeah!" she exclaims.

Just then, Agnes runs into the middle of the yard and screams, "Oh no! A dragon is approaching!"

All the kids turn to see Gru's pet dressed as a dragon. His name is Kyle, and he has long, spiky teeth. Kyle is not thrilled to play the part of the dragon and grumbles, causing the kids to scream and huddle around Agnes.

Then Agnes's oldest sister, Margo, comes out dressed as Joan of Arc. She is wearing a suit of armour and carrying a mighty sword.

"Fear not," announces Margo. "For here come the gallant knights!"

She gestures to a group of Minions wearing tiny suits of armour and holding different medieval weapons. The kids cheer as the Minions charge toward Kyle. But one Minion accidentally pokes another with his sword. A fight breaks out, and soon the Minions are fighting one another, rather than Kyle, the dragon.

Meanwhile, Gru is busy grilling burgers by the barbecue and talking on his mobile phone.

"No, no, no!" he screams into the phone. "What do you mean she's not coming? I have a backyard full of these little girls who are counting on a visit from a fairy princess!" He listens for a minute and then says, "I don't want a refund!

I want a fairy princess. Please! I am begging you!"

But the person on the other end of the line still says no.

Gru's voice gets low, and he says, "You know what? I hope you can sleep at night, you crusher of little girls' dreams!" He hangs up with a huff and turns to see Agnes standing in front of him.

"Ooh, ooh! When's the fairy princess coming?" she asks expectantly.

Gru stares down at Agnes's large, excited eyes. He opens his mouth to tell her the truth, but he just can't do it. "Any minute now!" he says instead.

"Yayyyy!" Agnes squeals with excitement and gallops off.

A worried look crosses Gru's face. *What am I going to do now?* he thinks.

He spots two Minions and instructs them to keep the children entertained for a few minutes.

The Minions get right to work, directing the kids to sit in a semicircle on the grass. Then the

Minions dress up as magicians and ask Edith to be their assistant.

Luckily, Margo is there to intervene. "Whoa! Whoa! Okay, all right. That's enough of the magic show!"

"Awww," the Minions and Edith say, disappointed.

Margo suddenly looks around. "Wait, did you hear that?" she asks the little girls. "It sounded like the twinkling sounds of magical fairy dust!"

The kids gasp and look around.

"It's the fairy princess!" exclaims Agnes. "She's coming!"

"Look!" yells Margo, pointing to the sky.

Up in the air is the fairy princess: Gru! He is dressed in a puffy pink dress, fairy wings, glittery eyelashes and a tiara, and is holding a wand. Edith's jaw drops at the sight, and the inflated balloon slips out of her mouth and flies up into the air.

Up on top of the house, many Minions struggle to lower the fairy princess down on a rope. But when Edith's balloon floats up and passes them, they get distracted. The Minions let go of the rope, and Gru swings wildly, smashing into the wall of the house before crashing to the ground.

"Aaaaaahhhh!" Gru screams.

Then he stands up and regains his fairylike composure. Adopting a high-pitched voice, he says to the girls, "It is I, Gru...zinkerbell! The most magical fairy princess of all! And I am here to wish Princess Agnes a very happy birthday!" Agnes beams with joy!

Gru sprinkles the other partygoers with glitter as they simply stare at him, frozen in their spots.

Gru says, "Okay! Time for cake!"

As the kids cheer and run to the table, Agnes approaches Gru. "Thank you, Gru-zinkerbell. You're the best fairy princess ever!"

Gru smiles. In the high-pitched voice, he replies, "You are welcome, little girl."

Agnes runs off but quickly returns. She whispers in Gru's ear. "I know it's really you, Gru. I'm just pretending for the other kids."

Gru watches Agnes join her friends. He couldn't be prouder....

Then Jillian comes into view. She is an annoying mother of one of the kids at the party and is always pestering Gru.

"Sooo...," she begins. "I'm going to go out on a limb here, but my friend Natalie is recently single and—"

"No, no, no, get off the limb right now," Gru says as soon as he realises what Jillian is saying. "No limb!"

"Come on," Jillian continues. "She's a riot. She sings karaoke. She has a lot of free time—looks aren't that important to her."

Gru shakes his head. "No, that is not happening. Seriously. I'm fine." He begins to walk away from her.

Jillian calls after Gru. "Okay, fine. Forget Natalie. How about my cousin Linda?"

"No!" answers Gru.

Just then, a Minion with his helmet on backward walks over and accidentally smashes Jillian in the shin with his club.

"Ow! Hey! Ow!" Jillian says as she limps away.

Gru is secretly grateful for the Minion. He just wants to relax and enjoy the rest of the day.

Too bad that's not the plan. Gru has no idea who's lurking just beyond the driveway. . . .

Chapter Two

A s dusk falls over the town, Gru takes Kyle out to the front yard. The creature lifts up his leg next to Gru's flowers.

"Kyle! No! Do not do your business on the petunias!" Gru scolds. He picks up Kyle and places him next to his neighbour's bush. "There you go. Those are Fred's. Go crazy."

Kyle does, and the bush immediately withers and dies. Gru chuckles. "Good boy."

A stranger's voice startles the pair. "Mr. Gru?"

Gru turns and sees a tall, redheaded woman standing there.

She holds up her badge. "Hi! Agent Lucy Wilde of the Anti-Villain League." She realises her badge is upside-down and flips it. "Oh, whoops!" Lucy clears her throat and changes her voice to a more serious tone. "Sorry, you're going to have to come with me."

"Oh, sorry, I—Freeze Ray!" Gru whips out his Freeze Ray and fires it. A wall of ice heads for Lucy.

But before it reaches her, Lucy pulls from her bag a Mini-Flamethrower, which instantly melts the ice.

"You know, you really should announce your weapons *after* you fire them, Mr. Gru," Lucy says. "For example..." She pulls out a tube of lipstick and fires it at Gru. The tip flies through the air

and hits him in the chest. *ZAP!* His body begins flailing in different directions before he finally passes out.

"AVL-Issued Lipstick!" Lucy calls out with glee.

Unfortunately, when she tries to load Gru into her car, he is a lot heavier than she expects. She finally gets him into the boot and is about to close it, when two Minions come around the corner.

Tom and Stuart see their boss in the boot and exchange horrified looks. "Boss!" they call out as the boot is shut and Lucy gets into the car.

The two Minions take off after the car, running as fast as their little legs can carry them. They

catch up to it and Tom leaps up onto the boot. He reaches his hand out to Stuart, who is falling behind.

Stuart jumps and Tom catches him by the strap of his overalls. Then the car begins weaving in and out of traffic. Stuart skis behind the car as sparks fly from his shoes. He runs into a clothesline and gets caught in a sheet, which turns into a sail and causes him to float! Lucy spots the commotion in her side mirror and slams on the brakes. Both Minions fly through the air.

Seeing this, Lucy quickly opens the convertible top on the car, causing the Minions to land right in the passenger's seat. Tom and Stuart strike threatening karate poses. "Hi-YA!"

Lucy zaps them, and they quickly pass out. She continues driving until she reaches a pier. But she doesn't stop! She drives right off the end of the pier and lands in the ocean with a splash!

The car transforms into an underwater vehicle as it submerges. Not long after, the Minions wake up. The vehicle speeds through the water, when suddenly an octopus slams onto the windshield. Lucy turns on the windshield wipers, which slap the octopus in the face until he's had enough and swims off, leaving an inky cloud.

"Whoa...," the Minions say in awe.

Lucy honks at fish, which part as a hungry shark comes right for them! She expertly steers out of the way just in time.

Finally, they arrive at a giant submarine with the letters *AVL* on the side. A hatch opens, and Lucy's vehicle goes inside.

Inside the sub, the water drains out from a holding dock. A hair dryer and buffer appear to dry off Lucy's car. The car is then lowered into a room filled with blinking lights and monitors, where busy AVL agents work in the background. As Lucy and the Minions get out of the car, she pushes a button on her keychain, and Gru is ejected from the boot.

"What...where...ah...foot's asleep...ah... pins and needles...," Gru says groggily. He realises he has a starfish on his head and a sea urchin stuck to his trousers and pries them both off. He looks around and has no idea where he is.

"Good afternoon, Mr. Gru," says a portly British man named Silas. "I apologise for our method of getting you here."

Before Gru can answer, Lucy pipes up. "I don't. I'd do it again in a heartbeat. I'm not going to lie. I enjoyed that—every second of it. Gave me a bit of a buzz, actually. It's like—"

"That's enough, Agent Wilde," interrupts Silas.

"Sorry, sir," Lucy says, taking a step back.

"This is bogus!" Gru declares. "I don't know who you people think you are, but—"

"We are the Anti-Villain League," explains Silas. He summons a map that shows all the AVL offices around the world. "It's an ultrasecret organisation dedicated to fighting crime on a global scale. Rob a bank? We're not interested. Kill someone? Not our deal. But you want to melt the polar ice caps? Or vaporise Mount Fuji? Or even steal the moon? Then we notice."

"First of all, you've got no proof that I did that," Gru says, his arms folded. "And after I did do that, I put it back!" he adds.

"We're well aware of that, Mr. Gru," says Silas.

"That's why we've brought you here. League's director, Silas Ramsbottom."

Upon hearing the name, the two Minions start giggling.

"'Bottom,'" repeats Tom, pointing to Silas's big butt.

Silas bristles. "Hilarious," he says, with a roll of his eyes. He instructs Lucy to continue with the debriefing.

"Oh, me now," she says nervously. "Um… recently an entire top secret Russian lab disappeared from the Arctic Circle. Yeah, the entire lab! Just whoosh! Gone. Where did it go?"

On a screen above them, an image of the magnetic ship that stole the laboratory appears.

The screen switches to show footage of a cute, furry bunny in a science lab.

"The lab was devoted to experiments involving PX-41, a transmutation serum," continues Lucy. "What is PX-41, you ask? Um, it's pretty bad. Look…"

Gru and the others watch the video footage of a lab technician approaching the bunny. The technician holds a syringe that contains purple liquid. As soon as it's injected, the bunny transforms into a hideous purple monster bunny! Then it goes crazy and attacks the scientist, the technician and even the camera!

"Hmm, you usually don't see that in bunnies," says Gru.

Silas's voice grows serious. "As you can see, in the wrong hands, the PX-41 serum could be the most devastating weapon on Earth. Fortunately, it has a very distinct chemical footprint. Using the latest chemical-tracking technology, we found traces of it in the Paradise Mall."

Gru skeptically questions, "A mall?"

"Precisely," Silas answers. "And we believe that one of the shop owners is a master criminal. That's where *you* come in." He looks directly at Gru. "As an ex-villain, you know how a villain thinks, how a villain acts."

Lucy explains the details. "The plan is to set you up undercover at a shop in the mall, where hopefully you'll be able to—"

Gru shakes his head and says, "Okay, I can see

where this is going with all the *Mission: Impossible* stuff, but no. No! I am a father now. And a legitimate businessman. I am developing a line of delicious jams and jellies."

Silas shoots him a look. "Jams and jellies?"

"Oh, attitude! That's right!" Gru says proudly. "So, thanks, but no thanks. Oh, and here's a tip: Instead of zapping people and kidnapping them, maybe you should just give them a call! Good day, Mr. Sheepsbutt!"

"Ramsbottom," corrects Silas, fuming.

"Oh, yeah, like that's any better!" Gru replies. He turns and heads for the door, followed by the two Minions. Gru exits AVL headquarters, which he now sees is on a submarine.

Lucy stops him. "Look, I probably shouldn't be saying this," she begins, "but your work as a villain was kind of amazing, so if you ever want to get back to doing something awesome, give us a call." She hands him her business card, which Gru takes.

Then he and the Minions row back to shore, wondering what on earth just happened.

Chapter Three

Gru gently carries a sleeping Agnes upstairs. Inside the girls' bedroom, he is surprised to find Margo texting and Edith out of bed.

"Hey, I told you guys to get to bed."

Edith changes the subject. "So when are you going on your date?"

"What?"

"Remember? Miss Jillian said she was arranging a date for you," explains Edith.

"Yeah, well, she is a nut job," Gru tells her. "And I'm not going on any date."

Edith looks puzzled. "Why not? Are you scared?"

Gru stares into space and starts remembering a time long ago when he was a little boy on the school playground. He was staring at a cute blond girl named Lisa, and he was totally lovesick. . . .

Unfortunately, Lisa doesn't notice Gru at all. She is busy chatting with her friends.

"Hey, did you guys see the moon landing on TV?" Lisa asks.

"Yeah, I can't believe it," replies one of the girls. "It's so cool!"

"And you know what?" says Lisa.

Before she can finish, Gru pipes up. "Excuse me, Lisa?"

But she doesn't notice him.

"I was talking to Billy the other day," Lisa continues to her friends.

"No way!" squeal her friends.

"He is soooo cute!" says Lisa. "And I think he likes me."

Gru gently taps Lisa's shoulder with his finger to get her attention. Then one of the other girls points to him and exclaims, "Ewww! Gru touched Lisa! Gru touched Lisa!"

The other girls turn and are horrified. "Ewwww!"

"Lisa's got Grooties!" shouts one girl to the entire playground.

The playground erupts with screams as all the kids turn and run away. A kid uses the seesaw to jump over the fence. Another kid hides in a rubbish bin! Two kids dig holes in the sandpit to hide.

Poor little Gru is left all alone, heartbroken.

When Gru comes out of his memory, he defensively stammers to Edith, "Scared? Of what? Women? No, that's bonkers! I just have no interest in going on a date, that's all. Case closed. I'm not scared . . . of women . . . or dates . . . . Let's go to bed." He tries to mask his discomfort by giving each of the girls a good night kiss. But when he gets to Margo, she is still texting.

"Whoa, whoa, whoa!" Gru says to her. "Who are you texting?"

Margo shrugs. "No one. Just my friend Avery."

"Avery? Is that a girl's name or a boy's name?" asks Gru.

"Does it matter?" says Margo.

Gru shakes his head. "No, no, it doesn't matter... unless it's a boy!"

"I know what makes you a boy," Agnes offers.

Looking concerned, Gru turns to Agnes. "Uh... you... do?"

"Your bald head," Agnes says confidently.

Gru nods, relieved. "Oh, yes."

"It's really smooth," continues Agnes. "Sometimes I stare at it and imagine a little chick popping out. Peep, peep, peep."

Gru stares at Agnes, both confused by and happy for her innocence. He sighs and gives her a kiss. "Good night, Agnes. Never get older."

He turns out the light and leaves the room, thinking one thing: Parenting is hard!

The next day, many Minions are at work in Gru's lab. What used to be the Missile Testing Area has now been designated as the Jam Testing Area. A series of contraptions push the fruit through different containers and onto a conveyor belt, where it is automatically poured into jars.

After being made fun of by Silas for his jam, Gru tentatively picks up one of the jars and asks his longtime mad scientist, Dr. Nefario, "So, how's the jam doing?"

A few of the Minions try it and almost throw up. They smash the jar on the floor and run away.

"Well, everybody's got different tastes," Gru offers, trying to brighten the mood.

Dr. Nefario sighs. "Listen, Gru. There's something I've been meaning to talk to you about for some time now."

A look of worry crosses Gru's face. "What? What's wrong?"

"I miss being evil," admits Dr. Nefario. "Sinister plots, large-scale crimes...it's what I live for! I mean, don't you think there's more to our future than jam?"

"Well, I'm also considering a line of chutneys..."

"Oh, you monster!" exclaims Dr. Nefario. "Evil chutney, I suspect?"

Gru shakes his head. "No, just regular."

Dr. Nefario is clearly disappointed by Gru's answer. He takes a deep breath. "Um...the thing is, Gru, I've had an offer of employment elsewhere."

"Come on, you're kidding, right?" says Gru.

Dr. Nefario presses a button, and his whole workspace folds up into a travelling suitcase. He is not kidding.

"It's a great opportunity for me," he explains. "Bigger lab, more evil, full dental..." He begins to sniffle.

Gru stares back at his old friend. "Very well," he says finally. "Let us give you the proper send-off."

Gru calls to the Minions, and before long seven Raspberry Guns are lined up. Dr. Nefario sits in his scooter.

"To Dr. Nefario, for your years of service," announces Gru. "The twenty-one Raspberry Gun salute!"

Seven Minions each blast their Raspberry Guns three times for a total of twenty-one.

Dr. Nefario begins to cough. His eyes water—and not just from the smell.

"I counted twenty-two." Gru looks down at Dave, who chuckles in embarrassment. And with that, Dr. Nefario pushes a button on his scooter, changing it to flying mode. He guns the engine, and it begins to fly away—at the slowest pace possible.

"Farewell, my friends! I miss you already!"

Everyone just stands there awkwardly as Dr. Nefario barely moves.

"This may take a while," he says. "Go about your business."

As his oldest friend takes off, Gru descends into a tunnel in the lab. He pulls out Lucy's business card and then makes a decision.

"You know what?" he says to his Minions. "Let's shut it down."

"We are officially *out* of the jam business!"

That night, Tom is dressed in a maid's uniform as he vacuums the carpet. There is a ring at the door.

He opens it and quickly backs away as someone throws a bag over his head and abducts him.

Another Minion wearing maid's clothes comes into the room and finds the vacuum cleaner moving by itself. He's not sure where Tom went. But he shrugs and goes back to work. The Minion abductions have begun....

The next morning, Agnes and Margo use Gru's laptop to create a profile for him on a dating website. Edith practices her ninja skills in the background.

Agnes asks, "Are you sure we should be doing this?"

Margo confidently replies, "Yes, it's for his own good. Okay, we need to choose a picture."

They go through a series of ridiculous pictures of Gru, each one more awful than the last. The final one is of him in a bathing suit. The girls scream in horror!

Just then, Gru enters the room, excited and proud to tell the girls the news about his job with the AVL. "Good morning, girls! I have an announcement to make."

But they are more interested in the dating profile. Margo asks, "Hey, what celebrity do you look like?"

Agnes thinks for a second, then says, "Humpty Dumpty!"

Gru sees Margo typing. "Wait! What are you doing?!"

Agnes parrots what Margo said earlier. "We're signing you up for online dating! It's for your own good!"

Margo gives her a *Don't tell him that!* look.

Gru freaks out. "What??? No. No, no, no. No way." He quickly grabs his laptop from them.

Edith pops down from the ceiling, startling Gru. "Come on, it's fun."

Margo continues, "And it's time for you to get out there."

But Gru's not having any of it. "No! No one is getting out there! Ever!" Then he quickly changes the subject. "Okay, now for the announcement: I have a new job. I have been recruited by a top secret agency to go undercover and save the world!"

This gets the girls' attention. Edith exclaims, "You're going to be a spy?"

Gru proudly declares, "That's right, baby! Gru is back in the game! With gadgets and weapons and cool cars...the whole deal."

Agnes looks up at Gru in awe. "Are you really going to save the world?"

Gru strikes a heroic pose and puts on a pair of cool sunglasses. "Yes. Yes, I am."

Chapter Four

Gru descends the escalator at the mall with three of his disguised Minions behind him. It doesn't take long to locate the cupcake shop, which looks like a small fairy-tale cottage with a big, plastic, pink cupcake above the entrance. The sign reads BAKE MY DAY, which immediately makes Gru frown.

"Blech," he says. But he knows he doesn't have a choice. This storefront will be his cover while he spies on the other stores in order to find the master criminal lurking within the mall.

Gru unlocks the front door and enters. Once inside, he turns to his Minions and says, "All right. Here is the cupcake recipe I got off the Internet."

The Minions excitedly grab the recipe and head for the kitchen.

"And don't go nuts with the sprinkles!" Gru yells after them.

Gru takes a look around and sees a bunny cupcake in a glass dish. Next to it is a shark cupcake. And next to that is Lucy!

Gru screams, which startles Lucy and causes her to jump up and hit her head on one of the shelves. All the cupcakes go flying! Using incredibly complex martial arts moves, Lucy dispatches the cupcakes as they come toward her.

She successfully destroys all the cupcakes, then turns to Gru, out of breath. "Whoa! Wasn't expecting that." She strikes a martial arts pose. "Or was I?" she adds mysteriously.

Then she sees that Gru has a cupcake stuck to the top of his head—icing side down.

"Oh…you got a little…here let me…," begins Lucy. She tries to clean it up, but as she wipes away a glob of icing, she just ends up spreading it more.

"STOP IT!" Gru finally explodes.

Lucy is surprised by his outburst. "Oh! I'll let you get it."

Gru wipes the icing off his face.

"What you just saw there was a little something new I've been working on," Lucy explains. "It's a combination of jujitsu, Krav Maga, Aztec warfare and krumping. It is not pretty, but it gets the job done."

"Well, the next time I'm a victim of a cupcake attack, I will know who to call," says Gru, slightly annoyed. Lucy stares him down. Gru then changes the subject. "Why are you here?"

"On assignment from Silas," explains Lucy. "I'm your new partner. Yay!"

"What?! No, no 'yay'! Ramsbottom didn't say anything about a partner."

Lucy shrugs. "Well, seems that because of your chequered past, everyone else refused to work with you. But not me. I stepped up. And I'm new, so I kind of have to do what they tell me, anyway."

Gru is about to respond when Dave the Minion comes out of the kitchen. He is carrying a cupcake shaped like a Minion.

"Voilà!" he says.

With lightning-quick reflexes, Lucy smashes the cupcake, flips Dave into the air and pins him to the counter. "Do you know this guy?" she asks Gru.

Gru stares at her in shock. "Yes, he's one of my Minions."

Lucy gasps. "Oh, I'm sorry! I should have known." She releases Dave. "You're free to go."

Dave stares at Lucy. He is instantly smitten. A magical glow appears around Lucy as Dave falls in love and imagines their future life together.

Gru's voice interrupts Dave's daydream fantasy. "Earth to Dave! You can leave now."

Dave goes back into the kitchen, never taking his eyes off Lucy.

Once he's gone, Lucy turns excitedly to Gru. "All right! Let's see who's got the purple stuff," she says. "Isn't it great? Secret spy stuff! Don't you love your job? Oh, this is going to be fun!"

Gru doesn't want to work with a partner, let

alone Lucy. His only response is a sarcastic "Yippee."

Chapter Five

A little while later, Gru and Lucy stare at a video screen from a hidden monitor inside the cupcake shop. They operate a camera that telescopes out of the cherry on the giant cupcake sign in front of the shop.

"A little to the left," Lucy instructs. Gru moves the camera to the left until he stops on an innocent-looking woman at a flower shop. "Okay, first suspect: Hedda Blumentoft, proprietor of Mum's the Word Floral Shop."

Gru takes one look and replies, "No, not her."

Lucy moves the camera to the next suspect: a small, perky man holding an empty teddy-bear skin. "That's Chuck Kinney, owner of Stuff-A-Pet."

They watch as he shoves the teddy bear's butt onto a metal tube. The bear inflates until it explodes into a torrent of bearskin and stuffing. Gru dismisses him. "I don't think so."

The camera moves again and lands on a short Asian man wearing a ridiculous blond wig. "Next, Floyd Eaglesan, owner of the Eagle Hair Club."

She pushes a button, and the camera zooms in on Floyd. He is standing in front of his store, waving hello to passing shoppers.

Gru jokes, "His only crime is that wig, right?"

Even though Floyd looks harmless, Lucy senses that he must be hiding something. "There he is! Twisted little sicko..."

Gru is frustrated at the lack of credible suspects and snaps, "Are we looking at the same people? Because there is no way they are villains!"

But before Lucy can respond...

Ding-a-ling-a-ling! The bell on the cupcake shop's front door rings, signaling a customer. Gru and Lucy quickly hide their equipment and try to act natural.

"*Buenos días*, my friends," a man says.

"Sorry, we're closed," replies Gru.

"Forgive me," the man says graciously. "I saw the 'open' sign in the window and jumped to conclusions. I shouldn't do that. Anyway...I am Eduardo Perez, owner of Salsa & Salsa Restaurant across the mall. Now open for breakfast!" He hands Gru a card. "And you are?"

"Gru. And this is Lucy. And now you may get out."

Eduardo protests. "But this is just going to take *un momento*. I am throwing a big *Cinco de Mayo* party, and I am going to need two hundred of your best cupcakes decorated with the Mexican flag. It looks something like this." With that, he rips open his shirt, revealing a tattoo of the Mexican flag on his chest. He makes it wave by flexing his muscles.

"So it's all settled," says Eduardo. "I'll pick 'em up next week. Have a good day. Come by if you get a chance, okay?" Gru is relieved when Eduardo finally leaves, but after a few seconds, he pops back in. "And welcome to the mall family!"

Because of where he is standing, the lighting creates shadows on Eduardo's face that remind Gru of someone. As soon as Eduardo leaves and the door closes again, Gru gasps and says, "El Macho."

"What?" asks Lucy.

"But it couldn't be...," Gru says to himself.

"What? What couldn't be?"

"That guy looks exactly like a villain named El Macho, from about twenty years ago."

Lucy listens intently as Gru explains the legend of El Macho.

"He was ruthless; he was dangerous," begins Gru, "and as the name implies, very macho."

Gru tells Lucy the story of how El Macho would drink snake venom and eat the glass it was served in...how El Macho headbutted an armoured truck and then punched through the bulletproof glass with his bare hands to take out the guards...how he then lifted the truck onto his back and ran down the street with it.

"Ah, but sadly, like all the greats, El Macho was gone too soon," continues Gru. "He died in the most macho way possible: He rode a shark with two hundred fifty pounds of dynamite strapped to his chest into the mouth of an active volcano. It was glorious."

Lucy stares at Gru. "Yeah, sounds like El Macho is pretty dead."

"They never found the body," Gru explains. "All that was ever retrieved was a pile of singed chest hair." He thinks of Eduardo. "But that face! It has *got* to be El Macho!"

Lucy excitedly proclaims, "Yeah, well, you know what? I say we break in to his restaurant! It will be my first break-in!"

Gru looks out the window and points to Eduardo in the mall. He is certain. "If anybody in this place has the PX–41 serum, it's him."

Chapter

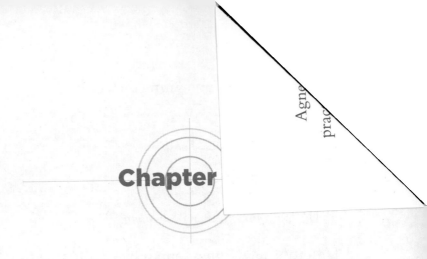

"All right, all right," says Gru, gently leading the girls into their bedroom. "Homework done, pyjamas on, teeth brushed, time for bed!"

"What's the big hurry?" asks Margo.

"I just...I have a lot of work to do," Gru covers. "So, hugs, kisses, good night, sleep tight, don't let the bedbugs blah-blah-blah..." He turns to leave, but Agnes is standing in the doorway.

"But you said you'd help me practise my part for the Mother's Day show!" she says.

Gru looks down at Agnes's puppy dog eyes. He grits his teeth and attempts a smile. "Fine, fine. Let me hear it—quickly."

is pleased and immediately begins to
use her part:

"She kisses my boo-boos.
She braids my hair.
My mother is beyond compare.
We love you, mothers, everywhere!"

Unfortunately, Agnes sounds like a robot when she says it, but Gru puts on a phony smile, anyway.

"Wow! That was something else!" cheers Gru. "I really liked the way you smiled at the end. Let's try this one more time, but a teensy bit less like a zombie, okay?"

Agnes tries it again, but still in the same monotone, robotlike way.

"Perfect!" says Gru. "Time to go!"

As he heads for the door, Agnes announces, "I don't think I should do this."

Gru stops and turns around. "What do you mean? Why not?"

Agnes looks at the floor. "I don't even have a mum."

At that moment, Gru feels for her. He tries to

cheer her up. "You don't need one to do this show. I mean, you were in the Remembrance Day pageant, and you haven't been in combat."

Agnes looks up at Gru. "This is different."

"Okay, well, then maybe you can just use your imagination."

"You mean pretend I have a mum?" asks Agnes.

"Yes, right," replies Gru. "You can do that, can't you?"

A smile crosses Agnes's face. "Yeah! I do that all the time! Thanks, Gru!" She gives him a kiss and runs off.

Gru watches her for a moment and then heads off to find his Minions, so they can babysit. He takes two Minions with him and goes off to meet Lucy.

But after Gru leaves, something strange happens: A light shines down from the sky right on two other Minions in the backyard. Before they can scream, there is a whoosh, and the Minions are sucked up into the air. These Minions have been taken, too!

Chapter Seven

At the mall, the stores are closed, and the food court is empty. As soon as the lone security guard turns a corner, Gru peeks out from his hiding place under a floor tile. After making sure the coast is clear, he whispers, "We're stealth ninjas. We make no sound."

Lucy appears next to him, and the two of them climb into the mall and quietly sneak up to the front of Eduardo's Salsa & Salsa Restaurant. Gru is about to kick down the door, but Lucy has a better idea.

"Nanobot Universal Key," she says, holding up a high-tech key. "Microscopic particles automatically arrange to open any lock known to man." She sticks the key in the door. It begins to make all kinds of weird high-tech noises!

Then it jams.

She jiggles the key, trying to get it to work.

Frustrated, Lucy just kicks in the door!

The pair walks inside. Gru is about to head toward the kitchen to look for the PX-41 serum, when Lucy stops him.

"Wait!" she calls. She whips out an aerosol can and sprays the air in front of her. "I'm checking for laser beam alarm triggers."

"It's a restaurant," Gru points out, annoyed.

"You never know what kind of booby traps this guy could have set," Lucy explains.

"There are no booby traps!" Gru insists as he takes a step, kicking a trip wire attached to a tiny bell. *Ding-a-ling!*

"Ha! Booby!" Lucy says triumphantly.

Gru and Lucy look terrified as the kitchen door begins to creak open, revealing...

A small chicken.

Lucy thinks it looks cute. "Are you lost, little guy? You must be lost."

Gru laughs. "Ha! Some guard dog!"

Suddenly, the chicken leaps into the air and lands on Gru, pecking his bald head.

Gru runs in circles, trying to swat the chicken. "Aaaaaahhh! Get it off me! Get it off me!"

Lucy thinks fast and grabs a nearby tablecloth. She lunges and covers the chicken with it.

"I got it!" she says, tightening the tablecloth around Gru's neck.

A muffled scream comes from under the table-cloth, and Lucy realises what she's done. She quickly removes the tablecloth and goes to karate chop the chicken. But the bird flies off, and instead Lucy hits Gru in the face.

The chicken clucks and attacks! Lucy presses a button on her watch, squirting foam onto the crazy chicken. The foam instantly hardens like a concrete ball around the chicken, with only its head sticking out.

Lucy jokes, "Hey, that *pollo es loco.*" Then she

sees that Gru is covered in scratches from the chicken and doesn't find her remark as amusing. "Okay, let's go."

They step into the kitchen, and Lucy pulls out a high-tech scanning device. She aims it around the kitchen and reads the levels on the screen. "Very interesting..."

"What is it?" asks Gru.

"I'm getting extremely high traces of tortilla," Lucy says. Gru rolls his eyes.

Lucy pulls out a pair of X-ray goggles and hands them to Gru to survey the kitchen.

Lucy comes into his field of vision. Gru freaks out because, with the X-ray goggles, she appears as just a skeleton. "Oh, that's an image I'll never get out of my brain!" He turns the other way and spots something behind a painting in the wall. It's a hidden safe! And inside is a metal canister.

"I knew it!" Gru declares proudly. He removes the painting, revealing the locked safe to Lucy. "The PX-41 is in here!"

"Then let's get it!" Lucy says.

Gru pulls out his own high-tech device and places it over the combination wheel. "This is going to be good!" he says gleefully.

CLICK. The safe opens, and a cold mist drifts out, revealing a metal canister with a label that reads EDUARDO'S SECRET RECIPE. Gru opens the canister. He sniffs inside and gets a concerned look on his face. He dips his finger in and licks it.

"Salsa?"

Meanwhile, Eduardo has returned to the restaurant. He senses something isn't right and scowls. Then he spots the chicken in the ball of concrete and gasps. "Pollito! What did they do to you?"

"Bawk!" cries the chicken.

"Who would do this to such a sweet little chicken?" says Eduardo. His eyes darken. He realises someone must be in his kitchen.

"I know you're in here!" yells Eduardo.

Lucy and Gru, who are devouring the delicious salsa, immediately freeze.

"He's coming! Hurry!" urges Lucy.

In the restaurant area, Eduardo grabs a knife.

"You coming out? Or am I gonna go in?" he yells to the intruders.

Gru pulls a laser cutter out of his jacket and aims it toward the ceiling. The laser fires and cuts a hole in it.

Eduardo shoves open the kitchen door, ready for battle. He enters just in time to see a pair of legs disappear into the ceiling. "STOP!" he shouts.

Lucy quickly pops down and shoots him in the face with the foam from her watch.

Eduardo wails in pain. "My eyes!" He drops the chicken, cracking its concrete shell, and tries to wipe the foam out of his eyes.

Lucy and Gru quickly run through the mall. Gru pulls out a device and contacts his Minions, who have been waiting in the car park. "We've been spotted! Come get us!"

A few seconds later, there's a huge crash! The Minions smash Lucy's car through the glass doors and speed through the mall. Gru and Lucy watch from a balcony above as the car heads for the escalators. Lucy sees the wreckage.

"Subtle."

They both run down the escalator toward the car.

"Over here, over here!" yells Gru.

But it's no use. The Minions don't hear him. They drive past them and back up the bumpy escalator stairs. The Minions are shaking and rattling. Once they reach the top, they make a left and start driving in circles. Gru pulls out a grappling hook and aims for the balcony railing.

"Hold tight," he says, grabbing Lucy. They shoot up and land right back where they started, at Salsa & Salsa! When the Minions zoom by in the car, Gru sighs heavily.

Just then, Eduardo emerges from the restaurant, wheezing and still unable to see properly. He is holding a knife in one hand, and he is out for revenge.

Gru and Lucy duck behind a cactus.

Eduardo pulls out a few kitchen knives and heads closer to the cactus. "I have you now!"

BAM! The car, with the Minions at the wheel,

strikes Eduardo. When he starts to recover, the car zooms past him—with Gru and Lucy hidden inside.

The car crashes through the mall again. Gru screams hysterically, but Lucy just hits a button. The car transforms into a jet. They fly off into the night sky. . . .

Chapter Eight

Gru and Lucy hide in separate bins in the food court, looking for their next possible suspect. They talk through earpieces.

Gru is still annoyed about last night's break-in. "I mean, who puts salsa in a safe? What kind of person does that? That's weird, right?"

"Very weird." Then Lucy spots someone in her binoculars. She whispers, "All right, there he is. Suspect number eight, Floyd Eaglesan."

Gru recognises him and sighs. "I told you, that's not the guy."

Lucy urges him on. "See if you can get closer. Go, go, go!"

Gru stands up in the bin, and his legs stick out as he makes his way over to Floyd. Just as he's about to get close enough to investigate, a man approaches the bin with a steaming hot cup of coffee.

Gru sees that the man is about to throw it away and quickly backs up. The man continues toward him. Gru backs up again. The man is determined and lunges toward Gru's bin with his hot coffee. Gru stands up and runs away.

Unfortunately, he doesn't see the escalator behind him. He falls down the moving staircase and lands with a thud. The bin pops off his head. Then he hears someone call his name. He looks up to see Margo, Edith and Agnes standing above him. Gru attempts a smile. "Girls, what're you doing here?"

"We thought we'd come visit you at work. So, you're saving the world in a rubbish bin?" questions Margo.

Lucy walks over to join them. "Hey, there you are. Oh, who's this?"

Gru introduces Lucy to his girls. Agnes stares at this new woman in Gru's life and asks, "Are you single?"

Lucy falters. "Oh . . . goodness."

Gru is also uncomfortable, so he claps his hands together to get everyone's attention. "Hey! I have an idea! Since Lucy and I have lots of work to do, why don't you girls go and explore the mall?" He quickly shuffles the girls away from Lucy. "Here is some money. Go buy some useless mall junk."

"Are you going to marry Lucy?" asks Agnes.

"Are you out of your gourd?" replies Gru. "No! She just works with me."

"On what? *Love?*" Agnes offers.

"No!" Gru tells her. "She is just my partner!"

"Plus you love her," continues Agnes. Then she begins to sing, *"You love her, you love her, you really, really love her, and you're gonna get married, and I will be the flower girl, and—"*

"Okay, stop!" orders Gru. "This is a song of

lies. I don't even like her!" He points to the mall. "Now go have fun!"

Lucy watches as the girls give Gru a hug and run off. Gru sighs in relief and walks back over to her. "Ha, ha, ha! Kids, right? They're...funny."

Lucy lets him off the hook. "Those girls totally adore you. I bet you're a fun dad."

Gru lets down his guard and can't help but smile. "I am pretty fun." Then he's all business again. "All right, let's get back to work!"

Lucy looks at the list of suspects and points to the Eagle Hair Club.

Back at Gru's house, an ice cream truck makes its way down the street. A couple of children run to meet it as it stops. But before they can, a mob of Minions rush out of Gru's house toward the truck. They shove the children aside and clamour around it, holding out their money.

"Gelato! Gelato! Gelato!" the Minions chant.

Suddenly, the metal ice cream cone from the

top of the truck opens up and begins sucking the Minions into it! One by one, the Minions disappear until there is only one left. He tries to make a run for it, but the truck lowers an ice pop in front of him. The Minion can't resist and licks it. His tongue sticks to the treat, and he is yanked into the truck!

As the vehicle drives away with all the Minions, the children look at one another with puzzled faces.

Chapter Nine

As the girls sit on the edge of a mall fountain, Agnes closes her eyes and concentrates for a few seconds. Then she tosses a penny into the water. She opens her eyes, waiting for her wish to come true.

Instead, Edith emerges from the water wearing a diving mask and snorkel. Her hands are full of coins.

Agnes asks, "Is that stealing?"

Edith answers coyly, "Not if my wish was that I would get a lot of free coins."

Margo sits nearby, busily texting someone, when something catches her eye: It's a boy! Suave, cool and a bit dangerous, he wears black skinny jeans and a black leather jacket. She watches as he strolls behind the fountain and then disappears in its spraying water.

Getting up, Margo goes to look for the mystery boy...and slips on a patch of spilt drink. "Whoa!"

The boy quickly appears as if from nowhere and catches her.

"Cool glasses," he tells her.

Margo laughs awkwardly, having never been complimented by a boy her age before.

"I'm Antonio."

"I'm Margo," she says nervously, as if she has forgotten her own name.

"I was just going to get a cookie," Antonio says. "Care to join me?"

Margo's stomach flip-flops. "Uh, sure," she says as casually as she can.

They begin to walk away together when Margo is reminded of her sisters. "I'll catch up with you guys later," she calls over her shoulder. "Bye!"

Agnes and Edith stare after their sister.

Edith makes a face. "Can I be the first to say *ewwwwww!*"

Agnes shakes Edith. "We've got to tell Gru!"

Chapter Ten

G ru approaches Floyd's Eagle Hair Club and adjusts a device on his belt buckle that scans for traces of PX-41. Lucy is in the cupcake shop monitoring the results. She talks to Gru through a Microscopic Transmitter in his ear.

"If it picks up any traces of the serum, the sensor in your belt buckle will make a sound like this: MEE-MO-MEE-MO-MEE-MO!"

Gru cringes at the annoying sound and says, "All right, I'm going in." He walks inside the Eagle Hair Club.

At the reception desk, a large chair shaped like

an eagle spins around. Sitting in the chair is Floyd Eaglesan, looking sinister and petting a furry object.

"It's about time you showed up, Mr. Gru," says Floyd.

Gru is startled. "You know my name?"

Floyd chuckles. "When someone who is follicle-challenged moves into the mall, I make it my business to know all about them. You are bald. And that is bad." He strokes the furry object, kisses it, and then places it on the head of a mannequin. It's a toupee! "There you go, my sweet."

Back in the cupcake shop, Lucy monitors the chemical-tracking device. "I'm getting nothing so far," she says to Gru through his earpiece. "I think you need to move around."

Gru hears Lucy and rushes over to a painting of Floyd flying with eagles. "Wow, this looks interesting. What is it?" Gru thrusts his hips at the painting, trying to get the sensor in his belt buckle to pick up something.

Floyd watches him, looking suspicious. "So . . . you're an art lover?"

"No serum!" Lucy says to Gru through his earpiece.

"Yeah, not so much," Gru says to Floyd. He zips over to a podium with a trophy on it. He thrusts his hips at that, too. "How about this impressive trinket?"

But Lucy tells him the device isn't picking up anything there, either.

Gru moves to a shelf filled with wig samples to investigate.

"MEE-MO-MEE-MO-MEE-MO!" Lucy's device has been set off. "Behind that wall!" she tells Gru. He moves the wigs aside and tries to see what is behind the wall.

Floyd picks up a sample. "These are my trial wigs. You should take one."

Gru is more worried about the PX–41 and responds, "No, thanks. So what's on the other side of this wall?"

Floyd gets annoyed that Gru isn't listening to him and snaps, "Look at me! Focus!"

Gru turns around to face Floyd, who starts his sales pitch. "Look, I know how tough it is being bald. The taunts can be so cruel. Chrome Dome, Egghead, Baldilocks…"

Gru shudders at each name as if he's been called them before. Floyd sees that he's now got Gru's attention and tries to close the deal. "I promise that this wig will transform you from ugly to irresistible."

Gru stares at the wig, getting caught up in what Floyd is telling him. He is about to respond, when Edith and Agnes burst in, both out of breath.

"Margo has a boyfriend!" yells Agnes.

"And they're going on a date!" adds Edith.

Gru's mouth drops open. "Date??? Boyfriend??? What???"

Still holding the sample wig, he races through the mall with the two girls.

"There she goes!" Agnes points over to Salsa & Salsa, just as Margo and Antonio go in.

Gru and the girls enter and see Margo and Antonio sitting together in the back of the restaurant. Margo laughs at something Antonio has said.

"Gross!" says Edith. "Look, they're in love!"

Those words hit Gru like a smack in the face. "Oh no! Do not say that they are . . . no, no, NO!"

Antonio and Margo stare at each other longingly.

Gru grits his teeth and storms up to them. Edith and Agnes follow close behind.

"And my dream is to one day play video games for a living," Antonio says.

"Wow. You are so complicated," replies Margo.

Gru interrupts them, trying his best to stay calm. "Hey, Margo, I'm totally cool with this situation, but could we maybe—"

Just then, salsa music begins to play. Across the room, a curtain opens and someone leaps out, spinning like a tornado. It's Eduardo! He lands with a flourish in the middle of the restaurant. He dances with customers and hands out business cards.

Not this guy, Gru thinks to himself with a groan.

Eduardo walks over to him and gives him a

big, warm hug. "So good to see you again, *mi compadre*!"

Gru tries to free himself from the hug as quickly as possible.

Antonio smiles up at Gru. "Oh, I see you have already met my father."

"What?! Father?" exclaims Gru.

"*Si!*" replies Eduardo. "Look at this crazy small world we live in, eh? Come. Sit. Let me get you something."

Gru looks down and sees Eduardo's chicken glaring at him. Eduardo picks up the chicken. Gru tries to pet it, but Pollito lunges at him.

Eduardo is surprised. "Oh, I'm sorry! Pollito is usually very friendly." He whispers to Gru, "He had a rough night."

The chicken gives Gru an accusatory stare. Finally, Gru can't take it anymore and says, "Well, we really should be going. Girls, come on." He tries to gather the girls, but Eduardo stops him, pushing Antonio and Margo closer together.

Eduardo sighs. "Young love. Is beautiful, no?"

"NO!" Gru yells, a little too quickly. He laughs

nervously. "You know, they're not in love. They hardly know each other."

Eduardo's face suddenly lights up. He has an idea. "You are right, *cabeza de huevo*! They must get to know each other better. Antonio, why don't you invite your girlfriend and her family to our *Cinco de Mayo* party?"

This sounds like the worst idea ever to Gru. (And he has no idea that Eduardo just called him an egghead!)

"No, no—" Gru begins.

"Si!" chime the girls. They are thrilled at the idea, as is Antonio.

Music starts playing again, and they all begin to dance. Antonio takes Margo's hand and twirls her across the floor.

From the side, Gru stares at Antonio with a look—a look that could kill.

Chapter Eleven

F ar away on a beach somewhere, the Minion with the ice pop stuck to his tongue wakes up. He doesn't have a clue where he is, but as he sits up, he sees hundreds of Minions—and they're having a party!

This is where all the abducted Minions have been taken!

But what the Minions don't know is this party is happening inside a large terrarium, being watched by a mysterious figure....

That night, at AVL headquarters, Gru and Lucy sit across from Silas.

"El Macho?" says Silas, fairly confused. "Hadn't we eliminated him as a suspect? After the whole salsa incident?" Gru shoots Lucy a look that says *You told him about that?* She shrugs.

"Yes, but there has been a new development," replies Gru. "I'm telling you, *this* is the guy. You need to arrest him immediately. And his deviously charming son. I'm pretty sure the son is involved, too. You've got to get the son."

Gru gets up and whispers in Silas's ear to make sure he's getting the message. "I think that the son is the mastermind. There's a look. There's a devilish look in his eyes, and I don't like it!"

Silas shakes his head. "But I don't really see any evidence for—"

"Evidence, schmevidence!" Gru says dismissively. "I go with my gut, and my gut tells me that this guy is El Macho. Lock him up. Lock up the son. Don't forget about the son. The kid gives me the creeps!"

Silas takes a deep breath and rubs his temples, second-guessing his decision to hire Gru. "Oh dear, oh dear."

Lucy jumps in, trying to remedy the situation. "On the less crazy side of things, uh, Gru discovered traces of the serum at the Eagle Hair Club." She shows an image of the reading on the serum detector.

"Hmm...interesting," Silas says, studying it.

"But it's not him. It's El Macho!" Gru says again.

"Mr. Gru, please," says Silas.

"No! It *is* him! And I will prove it!" Gru declares, and storms out.

Back home, Gru sits with his laptop, searching the Internet for articles on El Macho. Multiple matches pop up. *Ding-dong! Ding-dong!*

"Gru! It's Jillian!" a voice calls from outside.

Gru's eyes grow wide in horror.

"I have my friend Shannon here with me! I was thinking you two could get some grub. You know, tear it up! See what happens!" Jillian yells through the door.

Gru fills with panic. He sees Agnes skipping by and whisper-yells to her, "Agnes! Quick—tell Jillian I'm not here!"

Agnes nods and calls to the door. "Gru's not here!"

Jillian replies, "Are you sure?"

"Yes! He just told me!" Agnes responds proudly. Gru shakes his head wildly at Agnes, who looks confused. "I mean, no, he didn't just tell me!"

Jillian knows something is up and asks, "Agnes, where is Gru?"

Gru does a quick series of gestures at Agnes, trying to get her to tell Jillian that he's not home. But Agnes doesn't understand and keeps guessing like they are playing charades.

"He's putting on lipstick! He's swatting at flies! He's doing jazz hands!" Gru grits his teeth and clenches his fists in frustration. Agnes thinks she's finally got it. "Oh! He's pooping!"

Jillian has had enough and calls her final threat through the door. "I know you're in there, Gru! There's no getting out of this!" Gru sighs, realising he's going to have to go through with it. Then he spots the wig he got from Floyd.

Chapter Twelve

Gru and his date, Shannon, sit at a booth in a restaurant. Shannon has a fake, unnaturally orange tan and is dressed in a tacky leopard-print dress.

"I have to tell you," begins Shannon. "I was so nervous about tonight. I mean, there's just so many phonies out there."

Gru laughs awkwardly, as he is actually wearing the wig. He desperately hopes she won't notice.

"So do you work out? I mean, obviously, you don't. But would you consider it? Physical fitness is very important to Shannon," she says, vainly referring to herself in the third person. "You can tell, right?" She drops to the ground and starts doing push-ups next to their table.

"We are in a restaurant, you know," he whispers to her, feeling even more uncomfortable.

Just then, Lucy walks into the restaurant. She is picking up an order to go. Gru doesn't see her, but she sees Gru. She spots him with the wig and Shannon. "Gru is on a date," she says to herself. Then an idea pops in her head. She presses the button on her watch, which transforms into a high-tech eavesdropping device. She puts it in her ear and is now able to hear Gru and Shannon talking.

"Your accent is so exotic," Shannon squawks at Gru.

"Ah, well, thank you very much," says Gru.

"I know someone who can fix that for you," Shannon blurts out. "You'll be talking normal in no time."

Gru starts to sweat. "Ha-ha. Hoo! Is it hot in here?" He wipes his brow and accidentally shifts the wig on his head.

Shannon stares at Gru's hair. "Wait a minute. Are you wearing a wig?"

"What? I don't think so," says Gru.

"I knew it! You're a phony! I hate phonies!" exclaims Shannon. "You know what I'm going to do? I'm going to rip that thing off your head and show everyone what a bald-headed phony you are!"

Gru watches in horror as Shannon reaches across the table for the wig.

Back by the hostess stand, Lucy, who has heard everything, shakes her head. "I don't think so, Miss Lady!"

Quickly, Lucy pushes another button on her watch, which fires a mini-dart at Shannon. The dart goes into Shannon's bottom, knocking her out instantly—and saving Gru from certain humiliation.

Gru stares at the now-sleeping Shannon, confused. "Hello? Are you...?"

"Hey, Gru," Lucy says as she walks up to him.

He immediately removes the wig and tries to act casual. "Hello, Lucy. How you doin'?"

Noticing Shannon, Lucy says, "Wow. Looks like your date's out for the count. Almost as if she's been hit with a moose tranquilizer." She winks. "Yeah, I'm winking because that's what actually happened."

Shannon, still woozy, makes a loud moose noise, then passes out again.

Gru looks up at Lucy, realising what she did for him. He is impressed and grateful. "Well, thank you."

Lucy gestures to Shannon. "Shall we take her home?"

Gru nods, and together they carry Shannon out of the restaurant. When they get her into Lucy's car, it's too cramped with all three of them. So they end up strapping her to the roof as if she were a deer!

Once Shannon is on her own front porch, Gru and Lucy sit on the front steps of Shannon's house.

"Well, I think you did it. You just officially had the worst date ever," Lucy tells him.

"Humph, tell me about it." Gru groans.

"Don't worry. It can only get better from here,

right?" Lucy says. "But if it doesn't, you can always borrow my dart gun. I've had to use it on one or two dates myself. Well, good night, partner. This was fun."

Gru smiles as the word *partner* seems to mean something slightly different than before. "Yes, surprisingly, it was."

Lucy places a hand on his shoulder. "Oh, and, uh, just between you and me, you look much better bald."

Gru gazes at Lucy. Something is happening. Could it be? Is it possible? Is Gru falling in love?

Chapter Thirteen

*B*rrriiinnnggg!

Gru reaches out and turns off his alarm clock. He rises, puts on his bunny slippers, and is ready to greet the day. He hums to himself as if he has music bouncing around in his head. At breakfast, he serves the girls heart-shaped pancakes.

"So I take it the date went well?" asks Margo.

"No! It was horrible!" Gru says, and laughs gleefully.

The girls exchange looks. What?!

Agnes looks overjoyed to see that Gru is clearly in love with someone.

Gru skips out of the room and makes his way to work. He cheerfully strolls down the pavement. Passing a postman, he gives him a high five. He fist bumps a police officer. He stops traffic so a family of ducks can cross the street. He plays Ultimate Frisbee with a bunch of college students. He even joins a group of old ladies doing Tai Chi. It's like he's a whole new Gru!

At the shopping mall, Gru practically dances his way to the cupcake shop. But everything comes to a screeching halt when he sees that the Eagle Hair Club is closed. Gru spots Silas and some AVL agents walking out.

"Mr. Ramsbottom?" Gru says to Silas. "What are you doing here?"

"We got him," replies Silas.

"Got who?"

"Floyd Eaglesan!" explains Silas. "Our agents located a secret room in his shop last night and discovered this." He holds up a metal canister inside a plastic bag. "It's empty, but we found traces of the PX-41 serum in it. He's our man. So somehow, in spite of your incompetence, we solved this one."

Gru is stunned. "Ah...all right. So...now what?"

"Well, now you're free to go back to your *business*. Jams and chutneys," says Silas condescendingly. "And it looks like Agent Wilde will be transferring to our Australian branch."

"Australia?" Gru says, shocked.

"Yes," answers Silas. "But thank you for everything. And by everything, of course, I mean nothing. Toodle pip and cheerio, Mr. Gru." He walks away to join the AVL agents as Gru stares blankly after him.

"Hey there," says Lucy, approaching Gru. "So we got him."

"Yay, that's great," replies Gru, without much feeling. "And now you're going to Australia?"

"It's not definite yet," Lucy tells him. "Still figuring it out. Already been working on my accent: wallaby, didgeridoo. So...there's that..."

She pauses, awkwardly waiting for Gru to say something.

"Great. Well...good luck," Gru says, trying to hide his disappointment.

"Thanks. You too," says Lucy. Then she remembers, "Oh, I wanted to give you this." She takes out her AVL-Issued Lipstick and hands it to Gru. "Yeah, it's a memento. Just, you know, of the first time we met..."

Gru is touched by the gesture. He thanks her and takes it but is still too scared to ask her out. Then Lucy gets called away. After standing there for an awkward beat, Gru says, "Well...looks like they need you."

"Yeah, I guess...I should go. Well...bye." Lucy says and walks off.

Gru feels utterly miserable. He walks back home, completely depressed. He passes the college students playing Frisbee. He catches the Frisbee and tosses it down a sewer. He walks past the old ladies doing Tai Chi. As they balance on one leg, he pushes them, and they all fall over.

He sits on his front porch, feeling sorry for himself, and it begins to rain. Agnes comes out with an umbrella and hands it to him. He thanks her, and she sees that he is sad.

"What are you doing out here?" she asks.

Gru responds, "Well, you know when you

said I liked Lucy, and I said I didn't? It turns out...you were right." A look of excitement flashes across Agnes's face. But Gru continues, "But...it turns out she's moving away. I'm never going to see her again."

Agnes realises that her hopes and dreams for Gru to be with Lucy have been shattered. Ever the optimist, Agnes can't help but still encourage Gru. "Is there anything I can do?"

Gru looks down, depressed. "I don't think so, sweetheart."

"Well, is there anything *you* can do?"

Gru looks at Agnes and starts thinking that maybe she's right.

Not long after, he sits in his office. He is on the phone, reading out loud from a sheet of paper.

"Hello, Lucy? This is Gru. I know up until this point our relationship has been strictly professional and you're leaving for Australia and all, but, uh...okay, here's the question: Would you like to...go out...on a date?"

But Gru isn't really talking to Lucy. He's just

practising. Dave the Minion is sitting across from him dressed as Lucy, pretending to be on a mobile phone.

"Eh, no," replies Dave, in response to Gru's question.

"That's not helping," Gru says.

He looks at Lucy's card and turns to the phone.

"I can do this," he tells himself. He stares at the phone. It sits there, taunting him, until finally his nerves get the best of him and he bursts.

"Argh! I hate you!" He grabs a nearby Flame-thrower and melts the phone, angry that he let his fear of rejection stop him from asking Lucy out.

A Minion happily floats on a rubber ring in the fake ocean inside the large terrarium. He is about to eat a banana, when a mysterious stranger in the control room moves a lever, which creates a whirlpool that pulls the Minion down. The Minion is sucked through a tube to a chair, where he is strapped in with metal restraints.

He looks over to see another Minion eating a banana. They look at each other happily until a syringe of purple PX-41 lowers down next to one of them. It injects the Minion, and he starts to transform into a furry, purple, evil Minion! The other Minion laughs at his friend's misfortune until another syringe of PX-41 is injected in him, too.

Trying hard to take his mind off Lucy, Gru drives the girls up the winding road to Eduardo's house, where the *Cinco de Mayo* party is taking place. He pulls up in front of the open gate, and his car slams into other cars as he parks.

When they all get out of the car, there is red, green and white everywhere they turn. Sumptuous spreads of Mexican food are lying out, piñatas hang from trees and people are dressed in traditional Mexican clothing.

"Whoa! This place is awesome!" exclaims Edith.

As Gru turns around, he sees that Margo is

holding hands with Antonio. They are face-to-face, almost close enough to kiss.

"Argh!" exclaims Gru. He picks up Antonio and places him *far* away from Margo.

"Gru!" says an exasperated Margo.

"There must be a standard space of six feet between you and boys," Gru tells her. "Especially this boy." He turns to see that Antonio is already back next to Margo.

Antonio laughs. "You are a funny man. There are no rules, *señor*! It's *Cinco de Mayo*!" He faces Margo. "Come on! They're starting the dance!" He grabs Margo's hand and takes off, with Edith and Agnes following behind.

"*Arrrrrrriba!*" Agnes shouts excitedly.

Gru frowns and pursues them. While Antonio and Margo are dancing, Gru sneaks up on Antonio and grabs him.

But Antonio isn't going down without a fight. He stomps on Gru's foot and goes back to dancing. Then Gru pins Antonio to the ground. Antonio pushes Gru and trips him, sending Gru flying!

When Margo sees what's happening, she shoots Gru a dirty look as if to say, *You are embarrassing me!* and takes Antonio's hand, pulling him off the dance floor.

Gru skulks away, finding a quiet corner to sit down. He takes out the AVL-Issued Lipstick Lucy gave him and stares at it.

"So glad you could make it, *mi compadre*," Eduardo says, walking up to him. Sensing something is wrong, he asks Gru if everything is okay.

"Nothing is wrong," Gru replies, quickly putting the AVL-Issued Lipstick away. "I'm just chilling with the guac . . . from my nacho hat."

Eduardo puts his arm around him. "Gru, please. I can tell when one of my guests is unhappy. And I know that look all too well. It is the look of a broken heart, no?"

Gru opens his mouth to protest, but he can't. "How did you know?"

"Believe me, my friend, I, too, have spent many nights trying to drown my sorrows in guacamole. I know what it means to experience heartbreak.

To stay up all night wondering 'Is she thinking of me?' To want nothing more than to call her, but to be too afraid to even pick up the phone."

"Yes! Yes!" shouts Gru. "What is the deal with that? I'm not afraid of anything. And the phone is freaking me out!"

Eduardo shakes his head. "Love makes cowards of us all, *mi amigo*." He takes a crisp from Gru's tortilla sombrero. "But we are survivors. There's much more to us than meets the eye. Enjoy the party."

He gives Gru a meaningful look and then walks back to the party. Gru watches him go, trying to figure out what he meant. Then Gru notices Eduardo look around suspiciously and sneak through a side door. Gru gets up from the table and follows him.

Gru hides nearby and peers through a crack in the door, watching as Eduardo stands in the centre of a secret room. Mayan totem poles line the sides, and the floor is a series of lighted tiles. Eduardo strategically dances on specific tiles, making them change colour and play musical notes. Gru recognises the tune: "La Cucaracha." On the last note, a large totem's mouth opens and Eduardo walks into a lift.

Now that Gru is alone, it's his turn. He steps onto the dance floor and tries to remember Eduardo's steps. But as he moves, the guacamole from his nacho hat falls to the floor and lands on an incorrect tile. This activates a booby-trapped totem pole, which sends an axe flying toward Gru's head! He ducks quickly and it just barely misses him, chopping his nacho hat in half. Gru removes what's left of it and tries to dance out the code again. After several failed attempts, he manages to dodge the booby traps and finally plays the correct tune. The large totem's mouth opens, and he laughs in victory. He steps into the lift.

Chapter Fourteen

ucy sits and stares out the aeroplane window, feeling low. With a heavy sigh, she reaches for an in-flight magazine and opens it up. A headline reads "He's the One!" and shows a picture of Gru holding a flower.

"Say what?" she says to herself.

She turns the page and sees an image of Gru diving into the ocean with the headline "GRU!" She does a double take and sees it's actually just a travel ad with a random guy diving and the headline "GO!"

"Would you like some peanuts or pretzels?" asks the flight attendant.

Lucy looks up to see that even the flight

attendant looks like Gru! Before she knows it, she sees Gru's face everywhere. She knows she's imagining it but can't make it stop. She turns around and even a mum and her baby look like Gru! The baby Gru turns to her and says, "I just did a boom-boom!"

"I really need you to make a choice, hun," the flight attendant says.

Lucy finally breaks down. "I choose Gru," she shouts. "I choose Gru!" Then she runs to the exit door of the plane and flings it open. Air rushes into the cabin. "Thank you, Gru-stewardess!" she calls back.

And with that, Lucy jumps out of the plane. As she falls from the sky, she pulls a cord on her bag, and it transforms into a hang-glider.

Meanwhile, Gru and Eduardo shoot down in a lift. The farther the lift descends, the more nervous Gru becomes.

The lift finally comes to a stop.

Eduardo smiles. "I know who you really are, Gru."

The lift doors open, revealing an underground lair. It's a massive complex decorated in a Mayan pyramid theme. The magnetic ship from the laboratory heist is parked in the background. A long walkway leads to the lab section of the lair.

Gru looks around and sees Eduardo has quickly changed into El Macho's wrestling outfit.

"I knew it!" Gru says. "You're El Macho! No one believed me. But I *knew* you were not dead!"

"Of course not," agrees El Macho. "I merely faked my death. But now it's time to make a spectacular return to evil! Doctor, I think it's time we showed Gru what we're up to here." He gestures to the lab, where Gru sees the one... the only...Dr. Nefario!

Gru is dumbstruck.

"Nice to see you, Gru," Dr. Nefario says.

"Whaaaa? This is your new job opportunity?" Gru asks.

"Small world, isn't it?" replies Dr. Nefario. "You're going to like this."

Dr. Nefario pulls a lever, and the floor opens up. Rising through the opening is another floor, on which stands Kevin, one of Gru's Minions. Only it's a purple version of Kevin.

"Sorry, I had to borrow some of your Minions," says El Macho. "But it was for a worthy cause."

"Kevin?"

"No, he's not Kevin anymore," explains El Macho. "Now he is an indestructible, mindless killing machine. Just watch!"

Kevin eats an axe, swallows a police car and even devours an atomic bomb!

Gru stares, stunned by what he's seeing.

"Impressive, right?" El Macho says proudly. "And here's the best part: I've got an *army* of them!"

Lights turn on to reveal a lab full of kidnapped Minions in cages, and they have all been injected with the purple PX-41 liquid!

Gru can't believe his eyes.

"Soon, I will unleash them onto the world.

And if anyone tries to stop them—Yeow! Their city gets eaten!"

Gru nods, attempting a smile.

"And we can do it together," suggests El Macho.

"Together?"

"Together!" El Macho puts an arm around Gru. "I have admired your work for years, *amigo*. Stealing the moon? Are you kidding? We would be unstoppable! Men like you, men like me—we don't belong in cupcake shops and restaurants. We should be ruling the world!" El Macho holds out his hand to shake. "So, are you in?"

"Uh…yeah…probably," says Gru, trying to be as noncommittal as possible. He doesn't know how he's going to get out of this.

El Macho furrows his brow. "Probably?"

Gru realises he's in danger and quickly tries to backpedal. "I mean, yes. Yes! Of course, yes. I just have a lot going on right now. I just need to get some things off my plate before we start taking over the world, that's all. But I am like ninety—hmm—seven percent in right now."

"Excuse me?" asks El Macho.

"No, no, forget it! One hundred percent. I'm in!" Gru pretends to hear something. "Do you hear that? I do. That's Agnes calling me from the surface...." He quickly gets into the lift and frantically begins pushing buttons, hoping they'll return him to the surface.

El Macho stares after him, deep in thought. "You know what? I am not so convinced that he is in."

El Macho opens the restraints on Evil Kevin's chair and gestures for him to go after Gru.

Chapter Fifteen

Gru spots Edith and Agnes over by a *piñata*. Edith is blindfolded and accidentally hits Gru with the bat. Gru shakes it off. "We need to go home now!" he tells them. "Where's Margo?"

Agnes protests. "But I didn't get a turn!"

Margo is sitting at a table alone, looking depressed and wearing a nacho hat. She eats some guacamole and looks like she's been crying. Gru runs over.

"Come on, we're leaving!" Margo doesn't respond, and Gru notices that she's upset. He stops. "What's wrong?"

Margo points. Gru turns and sees Antonio

dancing with another pretty girl. Gru frowns and turns back to Margo. She tells him, "I hate boys."

Gru softens. "I wish there was something I could say to make it all better, sweetheart...." Margo appreciates his concern. She gets up and they all hurry off.

Gru quickly turns back and zaps Antonio with his Freeze Ray, surrounding the boy's head in a block of ice. Then he rushes to catch up with the girls by the exit.

Gru shuttles them into the car and takes off. In the background, Lucy is landing with her hang-glider. They just miss each other!

Lucy enters the *Cinco de Mayo* party.

She looks around but doesn't see Gru.

Suddenly, Pollito the chicken appears and flies toward Lucy. She strikes a martial arts pose, ready to defend herself against the treacherous chicken. As she does, her bag falls to the ground, and Pollito pecks at it, instead of attacking her.

El Macho appears, now wearing his regular

Eduardo clothes again, cooing, "Pollito! What's the matter?"

"Oh, hey, Eduardo," Lucy says.

"Lucia! I apologise," El Macho offers. "He's usually not like this. The same thing happened the other day with...Gru...." A realisation sweeps over El Macho. He has finally connected the dots.

Lucy has no idea, however. "Speaking of Gru, have you seen him? I really need to talk to him."

"Yes, I think he's somewhere around here," replies El Macho. "You two are close, no?"

"Oh, I don't know," begins Lucy. "Why? Did he say we are close? Did he say that?"

El Macho smiles wryly. "It's more what he didn't say. For instance, he never mentioned that you were both working for the Anti-Villain League!" He turns Pollito around, revealing that the chicken has Lucy's AVL credentials in his beak!

Lucy is completely unprepared for this. El Macho puts his hand on her shoulder. "You're coming with me."

Chapter Sixteen

G ru drives over his lawn and slams on the
brakes, stopping his car in the driveway.
Edith asks, "So Eduardo's actually El
Macho? Cool!"

He rushes the girls into the house. "Come on!
Everyone inside! Hurry up!"

As he enters the family room, red lights flash
around the big-screen TV. Gru and the girls turn
to see Dr. Nefario, looking nervous as he whispers from under a table at El Macho's lair.

"Gru! El Macho's on to you," Dr. Nefario says
hurriedly. "He knows you're working for the AVL.
And he's got your partner!"

"Lucy?" Gru says, his face falling.

Dr. Nefario continues, "He's out for revenge! And crikey, it's gonna be messy!"

El Macho calls to Dr. Nefario from offscreen. "Nefario! I told you to get that shark over here!"

Dr. Nefario looks at Gru nervously. "Sorry, gotta go!"

He quickly pulls a plug, interrupting the camera feed.

"El Macho has Lucy?" asks Agnes.

Gru gets a determined look in his eye. "Not for long." He turns to his Minions. "Let's go."

The girls watch them go, unable to stop themselves from worrying.

Out in the front yard, the girls' playhouse unfolds as Gru shoots out from a hatch below it on his Gru-cycle. Two Minions sit behind him and hold on tight as it rockets down the street.

El Macho's yard is now filled with rocket ships. His purple Minion army begins filing into the ships.

"The time has come, my Purple Army!" El Macho announces. "Today marks the return of El Macho! Soon the world will be ours! Prepare yourselves to make history! Today we will—" He looks at the Minions, who are kicking and hitting one another. "Pay attention to me! I'm talking to you!"

The Minions ignore El Macho and start tearing apart his home, using the pieces to smack one another around. Finally, he pulls out an air horn and gets everyone's attention. "Everybody back in line!"

Chapter Seventeen

Kevin, the evil purple Minion El Macho sent after Gru, has finally arrived at Gru's house. He walks onto the front lawn and eats a tricycle. Kyle barks at him, and he chases Kyle to the front door. Kyle runs away as Evil Kevin continues toward the house.

Inside, Margo and Agnes sit in the living room, playing a board game. They hear a noise outside.

"What was that?" Agnes says suddenly, clinging to her stuffed unicorn.

Margo stands up and walks toward the window. The curtains are drawn, so she reaches out a nervous hand and pulls them back. Margo screams. A scary purple Minion appears at the window!

SMASH! Evil Kevin crashes through the window and yells, "Blaaarghhh!"

Margo grabs Agnes, and they race out of the room. But Agnes accidentally drops her stuffed unicorn. She stops and runs back for it.

"Agnes, no!" screams Margo.

Agnes freezes when she sees that Evil Kevin already has her poor unicorn in his mouth. She screams a crazy, high-pitched scream that shatters all the glass in the room, including the glass in Evil Kevin's goggles. This confuses the evil Minion, so Agnes grabs her unicorn, and Margo grabs Agnes.

The girls run for the lift, with Evil Kevin close behind. The lift drops just in time, leaving Evil Kevin to smash into the glass door.

Down on the lower level, Margo and Agnes run into the lab. Edith is down there dressed in her ninja outfit and playing table tennis with her sword. Margo calls to Edith and the regular yellow Minions. "Quick! Help! It's coming!"

They shut the big steel door behind them. Phew! Nothing can get to them in Gru's reinforced lab. They are safe!

Crunch! Crunch! Crunch!

Evil Kevin has eaten his way through the ceiling! The girls scream and watch in horror as the Minion breaks through and drops down into the lab.

The yellow Minions all pile onto the purple Minion, but it's no use. Evil Kevin effortlessly tosses them off. He then stomps toward Agnes, Edith, and Margo, backing them into a corner. The girls look at one another, thinking this is the end.

At that moment, the purple Minion is injected with the purple serum. The Minion falls over and begins to smoke and bubble. Then he sits up and has turned back into a regular yellow Minion.

"Kevin!" says Agnes, recognising him.

Kevin smiles and waves, and the other Minions swarm him with hugs.

Margo looks up to see who is holding the needle: It's Dr. Nefario!

"Dr. Nefario!" Margo says, surprised.

"In the flesh and with the antidote," Dr. Nefario says.

Dr. Nefario produces a vial filled with yellow liquid antidote. He steps over to the vat of jam and pours the antidote into it. "Come on. Let's finally put this horrible jam to some good use."

In the meantime, Gru makes his way up the road leading to El Macho's house. He is wearing handcuffs and being led at spear-point by Dave and Stuart. They are painted purple to look like evil Minions.

They approach the closed gate. Dave gets on Stuart's shoulders and speaks evil Minion gibberish into the intercom. He hears evil gibberish in response. Dave shrugs and tries to respond in evil gibberish.

A green light turns on, the intercom buzzes, and the gate opens! It worked!

"We're in," says Gru. "Go time!"

As Gru and the disguised Minions walk through the gate, they get suspicious looks from the real purple Minions.

Dave and Stuart poke Gru with the spear.

"Curses! Foiled again," Gru says, attempting to act. "These guys captured me."

The evil Minions cheer. *So far so good*, thinks Gru.

On the long walk to the house, Gru, Dave and Stuart have to pass by crowds of evil purple Minions. Dave and Stuart are very nervous, but all is going according to plan. That is, until one of the evil Minions makes a slobbery raspberry at Dave.

Dave raspberries him back, trying to play along. Other purple Minions see this and think it's funny and join in. Soon Dave is covered in gross purple Minion slobber. He rubs it off, but the purple paint comes off, too!

They're exposed!

One of the evil Minions points and screams, and the others run toward Gru and the two good Minions. The evil Minions have their teeth bared, ready to chomp!

Gru knows there's only one thing to do: "RUN!"

Chapter Eighteen

G ru and the yellow Minions climb up a
tree to the roof of El Macho's house. It
seems like a great hiding place—but the
evil purple Minions are still pursuing them. Gru
kicks them away. But things are not looking
good.

Just then, Gru's ship appears, hovering above
them, with Dr. Nefario in the pilot's seat! Modi-
fied as a jam-dispensing weapon, the ship also has
yellow Minions hanging on to the sides, holding
jam blasters.

The ship opens fire on the evil purple Minions. One by one, they transform back into
yellow Minions.

"Hello, Gru!" Dr. Nefario calls from the ship.

"Hey! Nice work, Dr. Nefario!" Gru tells him. Then he and the Minions leap to the safety of the ship.

"I put an antidote in the jam," Dr. Nefario explains to Gru. "It's the least I could do!"

Gru nods his approval. "Thank you. Now, let's go get El Macho."

"You got it!" says a voice behind him.

Gru turns to see the girls on board the ship, holding jam blasters. Gru is flabbergasted.

"You brought the girls?" he asks Dr. Nefario.

"Yes," replies Dr. Nefario. Then, after a moment, he asks, "Was that wrong?"

Gru rolls his eyes, knowing that daffy Dr. Nefario doesn't really understand the concept of keeping children safe.

From behind a large jam gun, Edith unloads round after round. "This is the greatest day of my life!"

Gru changes his mind. Perhaps having the girls here *is* useful, after all.

The ship flies toward El Macho, blasting purple Minions along the way. Down on the ground, El Macho sees his Minions changing. "What's happening to my Minions?" Then he sees Gru and growls.

As the girls continue to take out Minions with their jam weapons, Gru tells them, "You guys finish dealing with those Minions. I'm going to find Lucy."

With that, he leaps out of the ship, down to where El Macho is standing. Gru has two big jam weapons of his own in his hands, primed for battle.

"Minions, get him!" El Macho barks at his purple Minions.

As the purple Minions descend on Gru, he smiles and says, "Let's do this!"

Meanwhile, Gru's ship lands on the ground below. The girls and Dr. Nefario storm into the battle. Agnes struggles to lift the large jam blaster. "Eat jam, you purple monsters!" She pulls the trigger and spins out of control, shooting jam at the purple Minions. Edith, Margo and Dr. Nefario blast their fair shares, too.

Gru transforms the remaining purple Minions in a slow-motion ballet of martial arts and jam. He approaches El Macho.

"It's over," Gru tells El Macho. "You've lost."

El Macho sees that all his purple Minions are now yellow again.

"Now, where's Lucy?" Gru says sternly.

"Let me show you," replies El Macho. He turns to a computer and pushes a button.

Steel doors open on the ground and out rises a rocket—with Lucy strapped to it! Tied to a shark! With one hundred pounds of dynamite strapped to her!

Lucy tries to keep it light. "Oh, hey, Gru! Turns out you were right about the whole El Macho thing, huh?"

A wicked smile crosses El Macho's face. "One push of this button, and I send that rocket straight into the same volcano where I faked my death. Only this time: It's for real!"

Just as El Macho goes to push the button, Dave swings by on a rope, knocking the remote control out of his hand. It flies loose, goes over the edge of the roof, and lands on the ground below.

"Noooo!" cries Gru.

El Macho faces Gru. "We could have ruled the world together, Gru. But now—you're gonna die." With that, he pulls out a vial of PX-41 and drinks it!

After a few twitches, El Macho begins to grow taller and hairier and also turns purple!

Gru and the girls gasp in horror at the El Macho monster. El Macho roars at them, looking unstoppable.

Gru tries to shoot El Macho with the jam gun, but he's out of ammunition. He quickly takes out his Freeze Ray and zaps El Macho's massive hands, encasing each one in a block of ice. El Macho laughs and smashes his fists together, sending pieces of ice everywhere.

Gru jumps to avoid El Macho's fists and falls backward off the roof onto a metal girder below. The girder falls, sending Gru to the ground. El Macho jumps from the roof and grabs the large girder. He swings it over his head, ready to crush Gru. Just as the girder is about to hit him, Gru quickly remembers Lucy's AVL-Issued Lipstick and uses it on El Macho.

A jolt of electricity shoots through El Macho, causing him to shake and dance until he finally collapses on the ground. He looks up and his purple fur puffs out from the static charge.

Agnes sees this and screams, "HE'S SO FLUFFY!"

Gru and the Minions surround El Macho, wielding their jam guns. El Macho says, "I am not afraid of your jam guns." Gru holds up Dr. Nefario's Fart Gun and replies, "Oh, this ain't a jam gun, sunshine!"

He blasts El Macho with the Fart Gun, causing him to pass out. Everyone cheers! El Macho has finally been defeated! One of the Minions jumps on El Macho's stomach and poses with his jam gun, like a hunter after a big kill. Another Minion snaps his photo.

Meanwhile, Gru runs to Lucy and climbs up onto the rocket.

"Don't worry about me, Gru," Lucy tells him. "I'll be fine. I have survived lots worse than this.

Okay, that's not entirely true. I'm actually kind of freaking out up here!!"

"It's okay," Gru reassures her. "I will get you out of this."

But he and Lucy gasp as they watch Pollito find the remote. The chicken looks at Gru and Lucy, then pecks the button.

"I *really* hate that chicken," Gru says through gritted teeth as the rocket blasts off.

While the rocket hurls through the air, Gru tries to cut the ropes with a knife. The shark is released, landing in an outdoor restaurant. The patrons and the chef cheer.

Up above, the rocket is still heading toward the volcano. Gru rips open a panel, revealing a mess of wires inside.

"Is there a red one?" asks Lucy. "It's usually the red one."

Gru starts pulling wires like crazy, but the rocket continues on. Gru realises he's not going to disable the rocket in time.

He looks Lucy in the eyes and summons his courage. "Listen, Lucy—we may not get out of this alive, so I need to know. If I'd asked you out on a date, what would you have said?"

Lucy smiles and replies, "Yes."

They stare at each other for a moment, and then Gru realises they are about to crash into the volcano. He grabs Lucy's hand and screams, "Jump!"

They plummet through the air and splash into the water below as the rocket hits the volcano and explodes with fire and ash!

Gru emerges from the water out of breath. Fiery balls of lava splash down all around him. He looks around but can't find Lucy! Gru frantically calls out to her, "Lucy! Lucy, where are you?!" Gru thinks he may have lost her, when all of a sudden she pops out of the water, gasping for air. Gru is incredibly relieved and swims toward her. "Oh, Lucy! I thought...I'd lost you."

Lucy lunges toward Gru and hugs him. They both go underwater. After a second, they pop up, sputtering—and in love. The Minions appear in a rowboat but accidentally pass right by them. Gru sighs and looks to Lucy. "They'll be back...."

Epilogue

Six months later, up on a hillside, four Minions dressed in matching suits sing their version of "I Swear." Only, they pronounce it "Underwear." Down below, Gru and Lucy slow-dance on an outdoor dance floor. He wears a tuxedo and she wears a beautiful wedding dress. All their guests sit at tables in front of them and watch, including the girls, Dr. Nefario, Silas, Jillian, Floyd and Gru's mom.

When the song is over, Gru playfully dips Lucy and tries to give her a kiss, but they end up bumping noses. After a few tries, they manage to get it right. Edith is grossed out. "Can I be the first to say *ewwwwww!*"

Next to her, Agnes looks around as if she has something on her mind. She takes a deep breath and stands on her chair, holding a glass of milk. She nervously clears her throat, trying to get everyone's attention. No one hears her, so Margo taps her fork against her glass of water. Everyone turns around to look at Agnes. Now that they are all staring at her, she's even more nervous. But she manages to squeak out, "Um…so…I'd like to make some toast."

Gru proudly nods to her and mouths, "Okay… you can do it."

This gives Agnes some courage, and she tries to pull herself together to say what she wants to say. She looks at Lucy and delivers a beautiful, personalised, and heartfelt version of her Mother's Day poem.

> *"She kisses my boo-boos.*
> *She braids my hair.*
> *We love you, mothers, everywhere!*
> *But my mom, Lucy, is beyond compare."*

Lucy loves it and runs over to Agnes, giving her a big hug. Gru, Margo, and Edith all join them. Agnes holds up her glass of milk and announces, "To the bride and Gru!" Everyone cheers and applauds. Their family is now complete!

Dr. Nefario turns on the music. Everyone dances back over to the hillside, where they take family photos. Agnes screams, "I'M SO HAAAAPPPPY!"

Then, just as the last picture is taken, an evil purple Minion pops up and photobombs it! "BLAAAGH!"

GREAT GAMES. NOW WITH EXTRA MINION.

That's right, kids. Minions have taken over your favorite games. There's only one thing to do...join 'em! Play **MONOPOLY:** *Despicable Me 2* **Edition** or **OPERATION:** *Despicable Me 2* **Edition** to have super-awesome fun, Minion-style!

www.despicable.me

Gru used to be the world's biggest villain.

Now he's a dad to Margo, Edith, and Agnes and has his Minions do his housework.

One day, Agent Lucy Wilde asks Gru to help the Anti-Villain League (AVL).

The AVL is looking for the thief of a very dangerous serum.

They suspects the thief is hiding in the shopping mall.

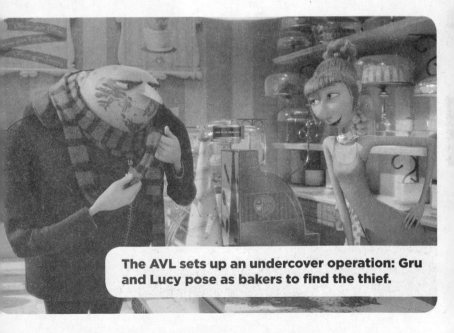

The AVL sets up an undercover operation: Gru and Lucy pose as bakers to find the thief.

Eduardo, the owner of the restaurant Salsa & Salsa, looks suspicious.

Gru uses his new spy gear to learn more about this man.

Gru decides Eduardo is actually a villain named El Macho, who would use the serum to destroy the world!

**But Gru wonders if Eduardo is really El Macho.
Or is he just a man who makes delicious salsa?**